Monsters

If you enjoy MONSTERS,
you'll love...

SPOOKS
WITCHES
VAMPIRES
PIRATES
SCHOOL

All published in this series by
Collins Children's Books.

MONSTERS was first published in
Great Britain in 1991 by HarperCollins Publishers Ltd,
77-85 Fulham Palace Road, Hammersmith, London, W6 8JB
First published in this format by
HarperCollins Publishers Ltd in 1995
1 3 5 7 9 10 8 6 4 2
Text and illustrations copyright
© Colin & Jacqui Hawkins 1991
The authors and illustrators assert the
moral right to be identified as the
authors and illustrators of the work.
ISBN: 0 00 198165-X
This book is set in Galliard 12/16
Printed in Hong Kong

Monsters

Colin and Jacqui Hawkins.

Collins
An Imprint of HarperCollins*Publishers*

Monsters

Beware the lonely road,
beware the dark forest,
beware the gloomy cave,
for here lurks...the beast;
hairy of leg, hairy of face, foul of
breath, shambling and loping of gait,
sharp in tooth and claw, beware the
creature of DARKNESS!

7

A good description you might think of lots of things that go bump in the night, but this ancient text relates to creatures that are always described in hushed tones as gigantic, fearsome, dangerous and wicked. Sometimes green and slimy with long squirming tongues; sometimes soft and squidgy with four eyes, six legs, and spitting poison and sometimes coming from outer space: they are MONSTERS!

Grrr!

* Typical monster greeting.

In this book we will explore the world of the monster.

Who were they?

Do they still exist?

Where do they live?

Do they have any friends?

What and whom do they eat?

Which are the worst monsters?

Do **YOU** know a monster?

All these and many more monstrous questions will be answered.

Hairy Scary and BIG

Huge hairy monsters with enormous feet live in the forests of Canada and America. They are called 'Big Foot' or 'Sasquatch' by the native Americans. In 1924 Albert Ostman was carried off by a Big Foot while he was camping, though luckily he managed to escape. He reported that the creature was about three metres tall, covered in reddish brown hair and had very big smelly feet.

30 inches (c

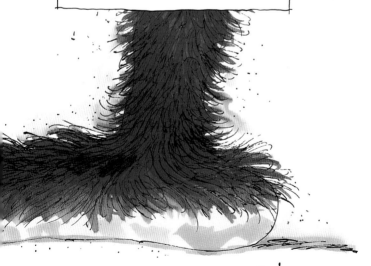

Do you know anyone with reddish brown hair and very smelly feet?

(¼ × the width of this page) ——— ⚡|

Woodsman Lore:- All they monsters 'ave an 'airy belly. Their feet are huge and 'orribly 'orribly smelly!

In Tibet they call the hairy giant the 'Yeti' or 'Abominable Snowman'. It lives high up in the Himalayan mountains.

You'd have to be sly
to see a Yeti pass by.
They live way up high
and are very, very shy.
(Old sherpa rhyme)

What do abominable snowmen love to eat?
Chilli!

The Australians call their monster the 'Yowie'.

Ranger Lore :- The Yowie likes
a booze.
An then he has
a snooze.

Howie Yowie!

Good on Ya roo!

A werewolf* is a terrifying sight: have you seen a man transformed into a ferocious wolf every full moon? There are several signs by which a werewolf can be recognised.

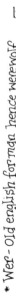

Werewolves are hairy and very scary.

Beware Werewolves

Father Werewolf to mother werewolf :—

Oh no. The baby's howling again.

Take a good look around you. Do you see anyone with eyebrows that meet in the middle, with small pointed ears, sharp fingernails and, the surest sign of all, hairs on the palms of the hands?

Are you weird enough to become a werewolf? If you are— there are various methods you can try.

Roll in the sand at full moon.

Eat wolfbane sandwiches for packed lunch or supper.

Drink from the same water as a wolf.

(Perhaps you could let us know if any of these work.)

Midnight Howlers:-

How does a werewolf brush its
hairy mouth?
  With a fine tooth comb.

Mummy, mummy, what's a werewolf?
  Shut up and comb your face.

Why did the Werewolf get indigestion?
  He kept eating people who disagreed
  with him.

I t was rumoured that King John was a werewolf. Norman monks heard sounds coming from his grave. They dug him up and re-buried him in unconsecrated ground.

King John was a hairy fellow, with teeth long and yellow.
His breath was smelly and really foul and every night you'd hear him howl.

St Patrick cursed an Irish family who had upset him. They became werewolves every seven years for seventy years.

The werewolf can be defeated by taking three drops of its blood, while it is still in wolf form. An easier remedy is to shoot the wolf with a silver bullet. Or, if you know his human name, call it out loudly three times. Failing all these – *RUN!*

In all the seas of the world dwell terrible, tentacled, squirming sea monsters and slippery, spitting sea serpents. They are the terror and torment of all those who sail the seven seas.

In November 1861, the crew of the French ship Electon battled with a huge sea creature. The monster eventually made off leaving behind an eight metre length of its tail.

How do you suppose
when a serpent grows?
He tickles his toes
and picks his nose?
No one knows.

In the dark and gloomy mist a sea serpent hissed...

I've just eaten up my brother, Now I'll go and eat up Mother

Sea Monsters

Old Mariner's Lore:-

Seaweed on the shore
Monsters will roar.

When the surf's white
Monsters will bite.

21

Watery, Weird and Warty

The best known of all the water monsters is Nessie of Loch Ness in Scotland. She is a dreadful, slimy, slithering Scottish reptile* with a long eel-like neck, enormous jaws and powerful flippers. Nessie emerges from the deep dark dank waters of Loch Ness to prey on American tourists who wear the wrong tartan.

*Possibly a plesiosaur.

In ancient times this terrible beast would drag foolhardy, hairy Scottish swimmers down into the dark waters of the Loch never to be seen again. However, in 565, St Columba commanded Nessie to be a 'Good Beastie' and thereafter she was, and left the swimmers alone (as far as we know).

In 1934, one moonlit night, a student called Arthur Grant was riding home, when he nearly ran into Nessie on his motorbike as she was crossing the road back to the Loch.

Old Monster Joke :- Why did Nessie cross the road ?
To get to the other side.

What do Sea Monsters eat?
Fish and ships.

What do you give a sick sea monster?
Plenty of room.

Most gigantic of all sea monsters is the Kraken. It is often as much as one and a half miles long and is frequently mistaken for an island.

Possibly the squashiest of the water monsters are the 'Globsters', shapeless warty humps of green flesh covered in hair. They are found on Australian beaches and are often called Bruce or Sheila. If they are trodden on they can be very dangerous especially if they go bright red.

Ancient mariner lore:-
When the Kraken awakes, an island it fakes.

Where did that come from?

G'day

Aussie Life Guard lore:-
If a Globster you should see watch your step and leave it be.

Baby Globsters will sometimes be caught by swimmers. They are known as Gobstoppers

G'day

Movie Monsters

Monsters are enthusiastic movie goers. They often go to the cinema to watch themselves on the big screen. They stuff themselves with monster-size buckets of popcorn, suck and slurp ice lollies, and guzzle big cokes. Have you ever sat behind anyone like that?

Movie Monster Lore:-
SCRUNCH, GOBBLE, GOBBLE, SLURP.
It all ends in a... BURP!

Hollywood has had many famous monster movie stars like King Kong the Giant gorilla. He terrified New York searching for his true love, the fair Fay Wray.

There once was a gorilla called King Kong
Who was so very big and strong.
He went for a walk and arrived in New York
And caused the most monstrous Ding-Dong!

27

Favourite Monster
☆ ☆ ☆ Movies ☆ ☆ ☆

'The Creature from the Black Lagoon'
'The Beast from 1,000 Fathoms'
'The Abominable Snowman'
'The Thing from Outer Space'
'Jaws'
'Alien'
'Godzilla'
'The Blob'

What do you do if a big hairy monster sits in front of you at the cinema?
Miss most of the film

Faster Wilber faster! It's gaining!

I know! I know!

28

THE BLOB

A jelly-like monster that blobs and
gobbles everything in its path, becoming
bigger and bigger.

'This film has lots of sticky moments.'
HOLLYWOOD PLANET

'A tacky ending'
FILM FUN

Why did Frankenstein's monster get indigestion?
He bolted his food.

Frankenstein

A nutty old German scientist called Dr Frankenstein was a do-it-yourself maniac. He built his dream castle on the Rhine as a bolt hole, then made his own monster with bits and pieces he dug up. Frankenstein's monster was a simple but kindly fellow with a screw loose.

Frankenstein was a lonely man until he learned to make friends.

Frankenstein's monster loved lightning – it gave him a charge!

What brings new-born monster babies to their parents? Frankenstork.

Why did Frankenstein visit a psychiatrist?
Because he had a screw loose.

Piz
Pi

Frankenstein's monster stepping out for two chilli and tuna and cheese and pepperoni take-away pizzas

I wonder why I'm a fly?
I don't chew the way you do.
I just suck. Yuk!

Heh! Heh! Heh! Heh!

'The Fly' is a horror film about a scientist who is half human, half housefly. This was caused by a fly getting into a teletransportation pod with the scientist. The result of this molecule mix-up was monstrous.

Why was Dr Jeckyll so hard to find?
He knew how to Hyde.

Dr Jeckyll drank a potent potion which turned him into the gruesome Mr Hyde. Mr Hyde was a monster with superhuman strength; he could see in the dark, had hairs on his chest, long white teeth and curly hair. Does your mum offer you potent potions and say, 'it'll put hairs on your chest'? BEWARE.

When space monsters glow
it's time to go.

Space Monsters

In 1952 in Virginia, USA, a group of friends investigating a bright flashing light on a hillside, were chased by a huge, floating, glowing space monster with bulging eyes and long tentacle-like fingers.

Space Monster Jokes :–

How did Martian monsters drink their tea?

With flying saucers.

Where do Martian monsters leave their space ships?

At parking meteors.

Space monsters are reported to have visited earth for thousands of years. In 1961 Joe Somontan of Wisconsin, USA, was visited in his back garden by little green men. They gave him a pancake, and said that it was their mission to seek out New Worlds, to go where no little green men had gone before and to start an Intergalactic Pancake Delivery Service.

Some space monsters are not so friendly. In 1954 a lorry driver in Venezuela stopped in surprise to see a strange unearthly craft hovering over the road. Small, hairy monsters with glowing eyes emerged from the spacecraft and attacked the lorry driver. He was then thrown over four metres through the air. Since then the lorry driver has been wary of the small and hairy.

Stranger than Strange

Deep in the jungles of Madagascar grows a tree with long tendrils covered in sharp spines. Its branches reach out and entwine unsuspecting picnickers, their cheese and tomato sandwiches and their smoky bacon crisps. Once snared, its victims are dragged into its dark heart never to be seen again. Never sit under this tree, it is the 'Man-Eating Tree of Madagascar'.*

*In ancient times Madagascar was known as the Land of the Man-Eating Trees.

Which is a monster's favourite ballet?
Swamp Lake!

How does a monster count to 100?
On his fingers.

Baa-zarre!

In Gévaudan, France, between the years of 1764 and 1767 the countryside was plagued by a wild beast. It was bright red,

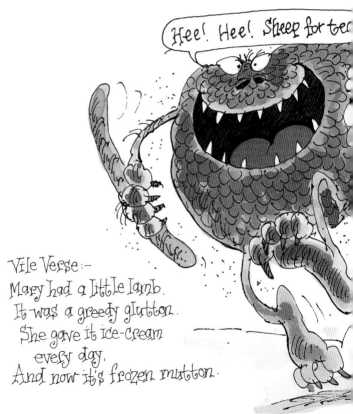

Hee! Hee! Sheep for tea

Vile Verse :-
Mary had a little lamb.
It was a greedy glutton.
She gave it ice-cream
    every day,
And now it's frozen mutton.

covered in scales, with a mouth the size of a lion. It was the terror of the local shepherds, carrying off sheep, tourists and croissants at every opportunity.

Monsterous Munch :-

Mary had a little lamb.
Her father shot it dead.
And now it goes to
    school with her
Between two chunks
    of bread.

Shall I tell you
a joke about the
body snatchers?

No, you might get
carried away!

41

Spooky Spider

Where do spiders play football? Webley.

What do you say to a monster with three heads? Hello, hello, hello.

Gobble Gobble

Isuchi-Gumo is a Japanese Goblin Spider with the terrifying ability to enlarge its horrible, hairy body at night. Could this be the original Little Miss Muffet?

What happened at the monster beauty contest?

They all came last!

What aftershave did the monster use? Brute.

How do monster children get what they want? By trial and terror.

Eeek! Horwid spidwer!

Monstrous Meals

Monsters are greedy gobblers, they believe in making a meal out of every meal time. They shove enormous quantities of food into their ever open, vast, dribbling jaws. Monster manners are dreadful.

On which day would a monster eat you? Chewsday!

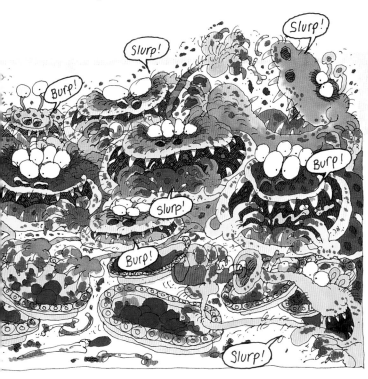

They slurp soup, chew with their mouths open, lick their plates, eat with their paws and put their elbows on the table. They never say 'please', 'thank you' or 'excuse me'. And they always burp.

Monster Menus

Breakfast

Vile Bile Juice (orange or lemon)

Weetabits (crunchy, wholesome
bits of anything)

Cold, lumpy porridge (for the hairy,
hardy monster)

Snap, Crackle & Belch (to wake you
up in the morning)

Musheli (for the healthy monster)
containing dried maggots, yoghurt coated
beetles, dried worms and lice flakes

Boiled Bad Eggs with toasted fingers
(dip and crunch)

Snacks

Blood Oranges

Yeti Yoghurt

Smoky Bogie flavoured crisps

Lunch

Snot Sandwiches with granary bread
Giant Giblet Burger (charcoal grilled)
Sliced Snake Salad
Snail and Salad Cream Sandwich
Tripe in warm milk (for the sickly monster)
Hot Thick Sick Soup (for the cold monster)
Croque Monstère

High Tea

Vomit Vol-Au-Vents
Snottage Rolls
Green Gilbert Gateau
Snail Slime Sponge Cake

Dinner

Spit Soup
Shepherd Pie (made with three
fresh shepherds)
Toad-in-the-hole with mashed maggots
Fried fingers with chips
Hot Potty Pie with Fried Lice
Squashed Fly Pie
Mucus Mousse
Green Mould Jelly with Frozen Eyes Cream

Monsters at Work

Even monsters need to earn an honest crust. Some professions have more monster appeal than others. Many monsters are attracted to teaching.

They often reach the top as headmasters or headmistresses, commanding respect mingled with terror.

Park keeping appeals to monsters. It is a healthy out-of-doors occupation with plenty of exercise, and the opportunity to meet lots of children.

Get off the grass!!

Eeeeeek!

First werewolf: I've just swallowed a big bone.

Second werewolf: Are you choking?

First werewolf: No, I'm being serious.

What did the werewolf say to his victim?
It's been nice knawing you.

Good evening

What kind of fur do you get from a werewolf?
As fur as you can!

What do werewolves do to cure sore throat?
Gargoyle.

Werewolves make dedicated night watchmen. They are physically well suited for this job as they can see in the dark and move silently.

Children who have nannies remember them well after they are grown up. This is not surprising as lots of nannies are monsters. Hairy monsters make super nannies as babies love to cuddle into their hairy chests.

Nanny Lore :-

Nanny knows best.
You'll get a cold on your chest.
Just put on a vest.
Nanny knows best.

I love my Nanny,
she's so weird.
Especially when
she shaves her beard.

She really thinks
it's such a lark,
to race me madly
round the park.

Worst Monsters

Monsters,
Rule OK!

Graffiti Monste[r]

Who scrawl
on the wall)

Monsters who never never wash and never never brush
their teeth.

Nnnngh!

Do you know
I've got bad breath
and BO?

Phe[w]

Litter louts who throw litter about.

E very worst Monster will always try its best to be the worst, when the worse comes to the worst...

Monstrous Old Jokes

onsters love to
cackle and titter.
Here are a few old belly
laughs and rib-ticklers.

Can a monster
without teeth
bite you?

Slurp! Sl
slurp! sl

No, but it
can give you
a nasty suck!

That's
right

Oh, no! Am I too
late for dinner?

Yes, everyone's
been eaten.

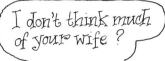

How should you treat a sick monster? With respect.

Sleep somewhere else.

What's big and ugly and red all over?

Burp!! Oh, Pardon me!

Poop!

Struth!

An embarassed monster

What's big, green, hairy and smelly?

A monster's bottom

Phoo! And how!

57

Monster

This little monster
went to market.

This little monster stayed at home

This little monster had roast beef.

This little monster had none, And this little monster went wee..wee...
all the way home.

Wee...wee...wee.

Monday's monster's fair of face

Aren't I pret[ty]

Tuesday's monster's full of grace

Pom! Pom!

Wednesday's monster's full of woe

Woe
Woe
Woe

Thursday's monster's got far too go.

I've a
long w[ay]
to go

Fridays' monster is loving and giving.

I love you
have my best bone

Oh, tha[nk]
you

Saturday's monster works hard for his living

It's hard work but I like it

But the monster that is born on the sabbath day is

bonny

I'm so bonny.

blithe*

I'm so nappy.

good and

I'm so good.

gay.*

Hee! Hee!

*Blithe: Old monster for happy

*Gay: Old monster for gleeful.

61

It is said that
any monster bits that
are chopped off a monster
will re-form into
a complete monster
again.

You have been warned.

Grrrr!

COLIN AND JACQUI HAWKINS create wonderful books
together. As they each do both the writing and the
illustrating, the way they work is a mysterious secret.
As Colin says: "What's spooky is that when we are
not together it doesn't work, and spookier still is that
when neither of us are there...nothing happens! The
nearest analogy is a visually-creative, brilliantly-talented
scriptwriting team of two."

Colin was born in Blackpool and Jacqui in Oxford
and they both studied illustration. They now live in
Blackheath, London, and have two children, Finbar
and Sally. When they used to read to their children,
Colin and Jacqui would add their own jokes and
humour to the stories. This desire to make children's
books funnier, together with their talent for illustrating,
led them into their current occupation. The first book
they had published was WITCHES and since then
Colin and Jacqui Hawkins have become two of the
best-known names in the world of children's books.